AVENGERS ASSEMBLE

Look for stickers that fit the shapes and activities found throughout this book. Use the extra stickers to decorate pages or make your own pictures!

POWER UNITED

MARVEL
marvelkids.com

© 2014 MARVEL. Published by Bendon. Printed in China.

55175 – **MARVEL AVENGERS ASSEMBLE - POWER UNITED** JUMBO BOOK TO COLOR

AVENGERS ASSEMBLE

The call has gone out and Earth's mightiest heroes need your help.
Assemble this puzzle!

HERO LOCATION — ACTIVATE!

Iron Man is using his super computer to locate the Avengers.
Help him complete the search!

The computer has located villains, too. Help the Avengers stop them.

AMAZING AVENGERS

Captain America needs to stop the
Red Skull. Lead Cap through maze.

START

FINISH

SOUNDS OF AN AVENGER

Find the Avenger who makes each sound in battle.

SFFT

CLANG

KRAKAKOOM

JOIN THE BATTLE!

Use stickers to create the scene.

HERO TIC-TAC-TOE

Grab a friend and choose the mini stickers that represent your favorite Avengers.

AVENGERS WORD SEARCH

Find the words from the word bank in the puzzle.
Look up, down, backward, forward, and diagonally.

```
B L A C K W I D O W
Y M T C I V O D L A
N I C K F U R Y A Y
N I N K R F I R C O
I F A L C O N T I D
A V M U Y E H K R L
T U N H C K W T E E
P P O H A W K O M I
A P R E Y E K W A H
C C I W B L O T R S
```

AMERICA	CAPTAIN	HAWKEYE	IRON MAN	SHIELD
BLACK WIDOW	FALCON	HULK	NICK FURY	THOR

THE AVENGING ARCHER

Complete the profile for Hawkeye,
The Avenging Archer.

WHAT'S MISSING?

Take a good look at the top picture. Use your stickers to add what's missing onto the bottom picture.

THE FINAL BATTLE!

Use stickers to create the ultimate battle for the mighty Avengers!

The Incredible Hulk likes to smash!

Iron Man suits up.

© 2014 MARVEL

Using the grid
as a guide, draw
The Hulk.

Captain America is a true blue patriot.

The Mighty Thor protects the people of Earth.

How many words can you make using the letters in:

● ● ● ● ● ● ● ● ● ● ● ● ● ● ● ● ● ● ● ●

MJÖLNIR
THE HAMMER OF THOR

_____   _____

_____   _____

_____   _____

_____   _____

_____   _____

Hawkeye never misses a shot!

Falcon soars with his holographic wings.
Nick Fury is the director of S.H.I.E.L.D.

Draw your own superhero.

BLACK WIDOW

How many words can you make using the letters in:
THE AVENGERS

_____   _____

_____   _____

_____   _____

_____   _____

_____   _____

_____   _____

_____   _____

_____   _____

Possible Answers: save, have, teen, hear, here, see, gave, has, ate, gate, get, set, rest, vest, are, anger, nest, hare, stare, than

HAWKEYE

THE
FALCON

Help Captain America find the Super-Adaptoid.

START

FINISH

Avengers Assembled

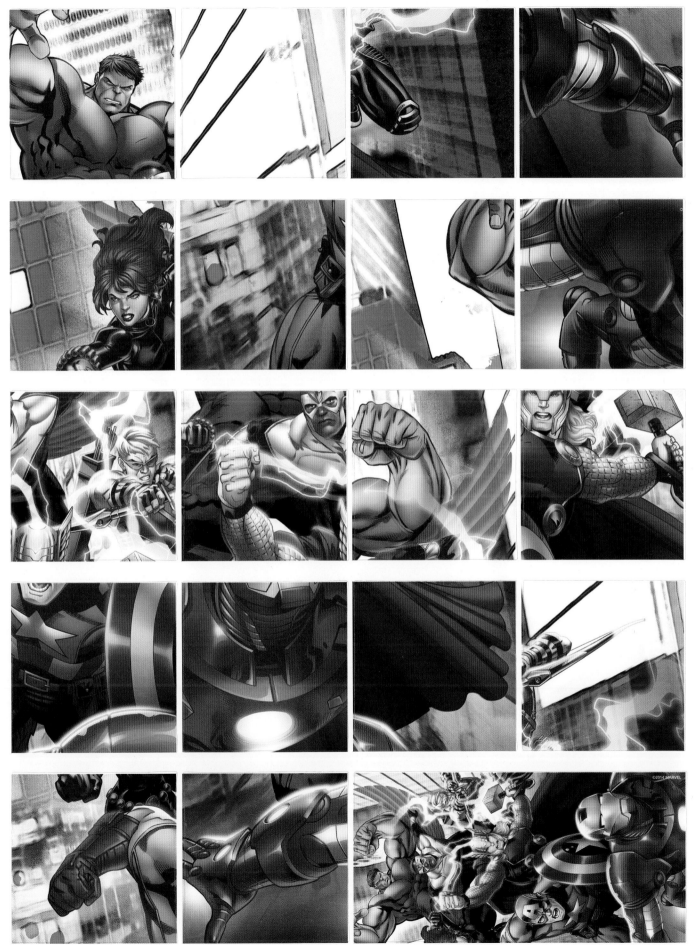